A Symphony of Whales

by Steve Schuch

illustrated by Peter Sylvada

VOYAGER BOOKS • HARCOURT, INC.

Orlando   Austin   New York   San Diego   London

AUTHOR'S ACKNOWLEDGMENT

Thanks to Dr. Antonovich Berezin, Dr. Roger Payne, and other whale researchers; to Diane D'Andrade
at Harcourt, Peter Sylvada, Jeff Dwyer and Elizabeth O'Grady, Andrea Schneeman, and
Marilyn Wyzga; and to all who have listened and cared.

Text copyright © 1999 by Steve Schuch
Illustrations copyright © 1999 by Peter Sylvada

www.HarcourtBooks.com

First Voyager Books edition 2002
Voyager Books is a trademark of Harcourt, Inc., registered in the United States of America and/or other jurisdictions.

The Library of Congress has cataloged the hardcover edition as follows:
Schuch, Steve.
A symphony of whales/by Steve Schuch; illustrated by Peter Sylvada.
p.   cm.
Summary: Young Glashka's dream of the singing of whales, accompanied by a special kind
of music, leads to the rescue of thousands of whales stranded in a freezing Siberian bay.
[1. Whales—Fiction.   2. Wildlife rescue—Fiction.   3. Music—Fiction.
4. Dreams—Fiction.   5. Siberia (Russia)—Fiction.]
I. Sylvada, Peter, ill.   II. Title.
PZ7.S4845Sy   1999
[E]—dc21   98-17248
ISBN 978-0-15-201670-8
ISBN 978-0-15-216548-2 pb

TWP   I K M O P N L J

The illustrations in this book were done in oil on gessoed board.
The display type was hand lettered by Georgia Deaver.
The text was set in Golden Type.
Color separations by Bright Arts Ltd., Hong Kong
Printed in Singapore by Tien Wah Press Pte Ltd
Production supervision by Sandra Grebenar and Wendi Taylor
Designed by Judythe Sieck

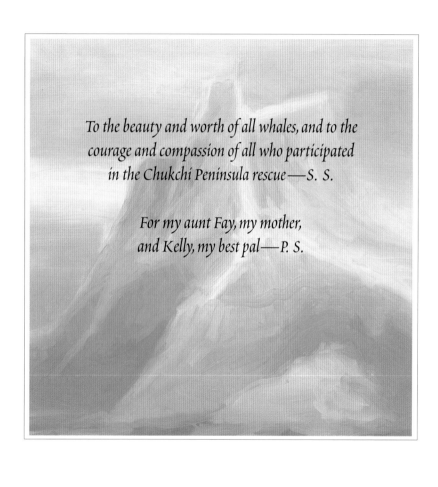

To the beauty and worth of all whales, and to the
courage and compassion of all who participated
in the Chukchi Peninsula rescue—S. S.

For my aunt Fay, my mother,
and Kelly, my best pal—P. S.

From the earliest time she could remember, Glashka had heard music inside her head. During the long dark winters, blizzards sometimes lasted for days. Then her family stayed indoors, close to the small fire. Glashka heard the songs calling to her out of the darkness, beyond even the voice of the wind.

The old ones of her village said, "That is the voice of Narna, the whale. Long has she been a friend to our people. She was a friend of our grandparents' grandparents; she was a friend before we saw the boats of strange men from other lands. But it is long now since one of us has heard her. It is a great gift you have." And Glashka would fall asleep, wrapped in her sealskin blanket, remembering their words.

The sea gave life to Glashka's village. The seals gave meat and warm furs to protect against the winter cold. In summer the people caught salmon and other fish, then salted them to keep for the hard times to come. And from Narna, the whale, the people received food for themselves and their sled dogs, waterproof skins for their parkas and boots, and oil for their lamps in the long winter darkness.

One year the snows came early. For three days a blizzard bore down on the village. When it finally stopped, Glashka's family needed supplies from the next village. Glashka asked if she might help drive the sled dogs. "It is not so easy to drive the sled," her parents said. "The dogs will know if you are uncertain of the way. But you will know the way home. Perhaps on the way back, you may try. Now go to sleep."

That night in her dreams, Glashka drove the dogsled. But the dogs did not follow her commands. Instead they led her to open water surrounded by ice. Glashka heard the singing of Narna, louder than she had ever heard it before. She awoke in the darkness of her sealskins, wondering what the dream had meant.

The morning was clear and cold as the family set out. The dogs made good time to the neighboring village. Before starting back, Glashka's parents packed the supplies into the sled. Glashka checked the dogs' feet for cuts. She rubbed their ears and necks. Glashka's parents gave her the reins. "We'll follow behind you. If your heart and words are clear, the dogs will listen and take you where you wish to go."

They set off. Across the ice, snow swirled as the wind began to pick up. Suddenly the sled dogs broke from the trail, yelping and twitching their ears. "What is it?" Glashka's parents shouted.

"I think they hear something," Glashka called back.

The sled dogs pulled harder. Their keen ears could pick up high-pitched notes that most humans couldn't hear. But Glashka, if she turned just right, could make out the eerie moans and whistles that grew louder until even her parents could hear them.

The dogs stopped short. They were right at the edge of a great bay of open water, surrounded on all sides by ice and snow.

Everywhere Glashka looked, the water seemed to be heaving and boiling, choked with white whales. Her father came up beside her. "Beluga whales," he said softly.

Glashka stared. "There must be more than a thousand of them."

The cries of the whales rose and fell on the wind as they swam slowly about. The dogs whined and pawed anxiously at the ice. "Let's hurry to the village," cried Glashka. "We'll get help!"

Glashka's father, though, knew there was no help. "They must have been trapped when they came here last fall looking for food," he said quietly. "There's nothing we can do to free them. When the last of the water freezes over, the whales will die."

But Glashka's mother remembered that an icebreaker, several winters ago, had rescued a Russian freighter trapped in the sea ice. "Could we call on the emergency radio? Maybe an icebreaker can clear a channel for the whales," she said.

Glashka and her parents raced back to their village. They gathered everyone together and told them what had happened. Glashka's father got on the emergency radio and put out a distress call. "Beluga whales, maybe thousands of them, trapped. We need an icebreaker. Can anyone hear me?"

Far out at sea, a great Russian icebreaker named the *Moskva* picked up the faint signal. "We read you," the captain radioed back. "We're on our way, but it may take us several weeks to reach you. Can you keep the whales alive until then?"

Some of the people from Glashka's village started setting up a base camp near the whales. Others set out by dogsled to alert the surrounding settlements.

Everyone came—young and old, parents, grandparents, and children. Day after day they chipped back the edges of the ice, trying to make more room for the whales to come up to breathe. "Look," said Glashka's grandmother. "See how the whales are taking turns, how they give the younger ones extra time for air."

As Glashka took her turn chipping back the ice, the song of Narna filled her ears again. She sang to the whales while she worked, trying to let them know help was on the way. Each day, Glashka looked anxiously for a ship. But each day, a little more water turned to ice. Each day, the whales got weaker from hunger.

Glashka knew how it felt to be hungry. The year before, her village had caught barely enough fish to make it through to spring. Sometimes the memory still gnawed at her. Even so, she gave the whales part of the fish from her lunch. The other villagers noticed and began to feed some of their own winter fish to the whales, too.

One morning Glashka awoke to the sounds of excited voices and barking dogs. The icebreaker had broken through the main channel during the night. "Hurry, Glashka," her parents called. Glashka pulled on her boots and parka and ran down the path to the water.

Everyone was gathered. Off to one side, the old ones stood, watching. They beckoned Glashka to join them. "Now," they said, "let us see what the whales will do."

The whales crowded together in fear, keeping as far from the icebreaker as possible. On board the ship, the captain gave orders. He hoped the whales would see the pathway cleared through the ice and follow the ship to safety. The icebreaker slowly turned around and faced back out to sea.

But the whales wouldn't follow the ship. "They may be afraid of the noise of our engines," the captain radioed to shore. "I've heard that trapped whales will sometimes follow the singing of other whales. We'll try playing a recording of whale songs."

Glashka felt a shiver down her back. "Narna's songs," she whispered to the sled dogs. "They're going to play Narna's songs."

Then the songs of the whales echoed over the water—deep moans and high whistling calls, ancient sounds from another world.

But the whales would not go near the ship. Again and again, the captain inched the giant icebreaker closer to the whales, then back toward the sea. But the whales stayed as far away as they could.

"It's no use," the captain radioed in despair. "And we can't stay beyond tomorrow. Already the channel is starting to refreeze!"

Glashka was near tears as she asked the old ones what could be done now. "Wait," they said. "Let us see what tomorrow brings."

That night the song of Narna came to Glashka again. Only this time it was different. She heard the music and voices of whales, but she heard other music, too . . . melodies she'd never heard before. . . . While it was still dark, Glashka woke her parents. "I've heard Narna again," she said. "And I've heard other music, too!"

"You have to tell the old ones," Glashka's parents said.

The old ones of the village listened carefully as Glashka told them what she had heard. "So, it is other music Narna is asking for," they said thoughtfully. "Long is the time, but once, it is said, humans and whales made music together. Perhaps the time has come again. Let us speak with the captain!"

Quickly Glashka and the old ones radioed the ship. "Have you any other music, people music, to play for the whales?" they asked. The captain said he would see what his crew could find.

First they tried playing rock and roll. The electric guitars and drums boomed, but the whales would not follow the ship.

Next the crew tried Russian folk music. It was softer, with many voices singing together. The whales swam a little closer, but still they would not follow the ship.

On shore, Glashka ran back to the radio transmitter. She had to talk with the captain. "I *know* there's other music that will work. Please keep trying!" she told him.

The crew found some classical music. First the sweet sounds of violins and violas, next the deeper notes of the cellos and, deepest of all, the string basses . . . and way up high, a solo violin. . . .

Everyone fell silent as the melody carried over the water. The whales grew quiet, too, listening.

A few whales started to sing back to the ship, and to each other. Gradually more whales joined in.

Then . . . they began to swim toward the ship!

Cautiously the captain started the huge engines and headed slowly out to sea. One whale followed, then another, then a few more. Soon all the whales were following the ship through the narrow channel, past the broken chunks of ice, back to the safety of the open ocean.

On shore, people laughed and cried and hugged each other. The sled dogs jumped up and barked, trying to lick the noses and faces of anyone they could reach. Glashka buried her wet face in the fur of the dogs' necks. "Such good, good dogs," she told them over and over. "Such good dogs. Now the whales are going home!"

On board the ship, the captain and his crew raised every flag. The music played as the captain radioed to say the whales were safe. He and his crew were finally going home, too.

Glashka and her family looked out to sea. They waved to the icebreaker and the disappearing whales. "And do you hear Narna singing now?" her grandmother asked.

"Yes," Glashka said, "but it isn't just Narna I hear now. It's something bigger than that . . . something like a whole symphony of whales!"

HISTORICAL NOTES

This tale was inspired by a true story. In the winter of 1984–1985, nearly three thousand beluga whales were found trapped in the Senyavina Strait of Siberia, a narrow body of water across the Bering Strait from Alaska. With the bitter cold, the water was freezing rapidly. In places the sea ice was twelve feet thick. For seven weeks, the people of the Chukchi Peninsula and the crew of the icebreaker *Moskva* risked their lives to save those whales. Against all odds, they succeeded.

There are several other recorded instances of rescuers leading trapped whales to safety by playing whale songs. But to my knowledge, the Chukchi rescue was the first time whales ever followed an icebreaker playing classical music. Was it Beethoven? Or Mozart? Or Tchaikovsky? The Soviet newspaper accounts don't say. That part of the story is still untold.

—*Steve Schuch*